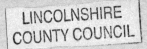
"At Christmas, I no more desire a rose
Than wish a snow in May's new-fangled mirth;
But like of each thing that in season grows."

William Shakespeare

Raphaël Thierry

Merry Christmas

a Superdog adventure

Andersen Press
London

"Hey, you've got a surprise coming!"
"Who, me?"

"Yes, you! It's Christmas!"

But what could it be?

Perhaps a new collar?

Or a new post?

Or maybe a nice soft bed?

Or just a few friends . . .

. . . to have a good howl with!

Actually, I wouldn't mind a bit of freedom!

. . .

"Merry Christmas!"
cried a voice from above.

. . .

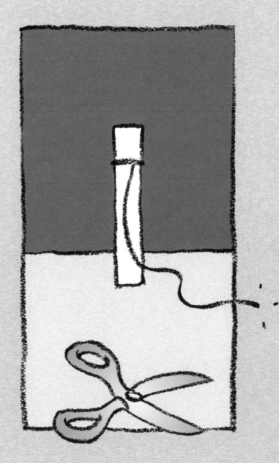

Hey, I'm still here!

It's true! Superdog is just too attached to his post!

© Éditions Magnard, 2001 - Paris.
English translation © Raphaël Thierry and Jeffrey Paul Kearney, 2004
First published in 2001 by Éditions Magnard under the title
Joyeux Noël - une aventure de Superchien.
First published in Great Britain in 2004 by Andersen Press, 20 Vauxhall Bridge Road,
London SW1V 2SA. Published in Australia by Random House Australia Pty.,
20 Alfred Street, Milsons Point, Sydney, NSW 2061. All rights reserved.
Printed and bound in Singapore

10   9   8   7   6   5   4   3   2   1

British Library Cataloguing in Publication Data available
ISBN 1 84270 419 2